THE CROSSINGS

†

Jack Ketchum

Jack Ketchum [signature]

THE
CROSSIN

THE CROSSINGS

Jack Ketchum

CEMETERY DANCE PUBLICATIONS

Baltimore

❖ 2003 ❖

Signed Hardcover Edition   ISBN 1-58767-067-4

Cemetery Dance Publications
132-B Industry Lane
Unit 7
Forest Hill, Maryland 21050
E-mail: info@cemeterydance.com

www.cemeterydance.com

"Mommas, don't let your babies
grow up to be cowboys . . . "

—Ed and Patsy Bruce

ONE

Here is what she told Hart and Mother and me about how it began.

She said it was the noise.

Said that the chickens were so loud clamouring for their morning meal that Elena never heard the horses' hooves over the din inside the barn.

She had always hated chickens and now she had them to thank for all the rest of it.

Sleepy-eyed this morning like any other she had watched them swarm across the floor of the barn and tossed the feed from the bucket out the door to lure them outside and watched them flow like lava into the yard and thought as she sometimes did that they were more akin to ants than anything else she had observed in nature or perhaps like darting schools of fish feeding in the river. Though no ant or minnow would ever stink as they did. That they depended upon her amazed her in some way. They were quick and moved with violence and their eyes were cold. How and why creatures this fierce had come to the reduced state of pensioners disgusted her.

She by then had called out twice for her sister Celine to come gather the eggs but Celine was young and lazy mornings and she had to call again before she saw the door flung open and her sister appear in the doorway, pretty and half-asleep and petulant looking so that despite her annoyance Elena had to smile. The door slammed shut and she watched her father behind the cloudy window pulling up his suspenders, glancing at them and turning away.

She passed her sister wordlessly in the yard and as Celine disappeared into the barn spread the last of her feed in a series of wide arcs from the heavy old bucket and then headed for the house and that was when she saw them riding toward her just outside the yard.

Four men. The horses young and strong.

Three of the men Mexican. The fourth Anglo. All of them filthy with the dust and sweat of travel. Armed with rifles, pistols. Bandoliers slung across their chests.

Warriors, she thought.

Their presence frightened and angered her. The huge bald Anglo especially who watched her deliberately with grey eyes unwavering as he rode through the sea of chickens scattering them beneath his horse's hooves until he was close enough so that she could see the livid scar, the letter *D* branded across his cheek from jaw to cheekbone and back again.

To hell with you, she thought and returned his gaze. *We have had enough of war.*

She heard the Mexicans laugh as they giddied their horses into the yard maddening the chickens and perhaps the horses too unused to so many small creatures darting under and away beneath their feet so that they bucked and whinnied. She heard the slide of rifle out of scabbard and saw the tall thin one with the Indio blood like her dead mother's blood raise his carbine and fire into the hardpack and saw dirt fly and the man fire again and this time where once there was a chicken there was now only some headless wingless carcass clawing toward its end.

It happened very fast then.

Except for the Anglo who remained calm and still all of them began firing riding into the chickens shouting *comida! comida!* yet creating more confusion than damage to the birds. She saw Celine peer out from the barn at the gunfire and dart back in again but not before the fat one she would later know as Fredo noticed her and rode inside. She glanced at the window and saw her father and watched him turn away and knew he had gone for his rifle.

When the fat one rode out of the barn he had Celine up astride the saddlehorn in front of him squirming and kicking and trying to scratch. The man was laughing. So were his friends. Even the Anglo was smiling. She took three steps forward and swung the heavy wooden bucket at the back of the fat man's head and heard a sound like a stone dropped into a deep dry well and felt the impact all the way up to her shoulder and with great satisfaction saw blood fly.

The man howled and dropped her sister to the ground and only a lunge for his saddlehorn prevented him from falling but she said it was exactly then that her father appeared in the doorway and the Anglo drew and fired four times in rapid succession. Her father fell back through the doorway with a bullet in his forehead and his blood arced high across the old wooden lintel.

† †

She didn't tell us what she felt just then and we didn't ask. There hardly seemed any need. It was the night before we crossed the Colorado and her face glowing in the light from the campfire had the look of something ancient wrought from carved and polished stone. We ate beans and salt beef and bread and rattlesnake and it was the first she'd really talked to us and even Mother was mostly silent for a change.

† †

She said she asked the Anglo his name and he told her.
She said, "take your chickens and go, Paddy Ryan."
And he said, "thanks, we will."
They got down off their horses and that was when they had them first, right there among the chickens in the yard.

TWO

John Charles Hart and I met in 1848, the year the Mexican war ended, in what later would be called Arizona, in a grown-overnight booming little town called Gable's Ferry just across the Colorado River from the California gold fields north and Mexico to the south. I was drunk and barely twenty-one and Hart was playing cards with two other men in the Little Fanny Saloon. I'd seen him in there nearly every night but we'd never spoken a word to one another.

Were it not for the gold at Sutter's Mill that January neither the Little Fanny nor the town for that matter would have had reason to exist. It certainly wasn't Mexico that drew the bulk of those pilgrims. But there was a narrows in the river there that made it a natural place for a ferry so an old roughneck named Gable had built one and manned it with his shotgun and a pair of well-trained dogs. Just a primitive barge-and-cable affair that you knew the river would swallow whole come flood time but for now it did what it was supposed to do and word had got around.

I'd been there pretty nearly from its inception. I'd seen barrels of whiskey and billiard tables come in and fancy wear and ready-made clothing, card sharks and whores and trappers and tradesmen and miners pouring through each day. Within a month or so we had a makeshift saloon and whorehouse, a dry goods store and another saloon, a stable and a grocery. Everything in fact except a church, a schoolhouse and a jail.

Though most would maintain that only the last was needed.

Prices had gone mad. Across the river inexperienced miners were pulling a hundred twenty-five dollars a day and everyone knew it. At Gable's Ferry you could pitch a tent, set some cots inside and charge a dollar a night lodging and plenty of men were willing to pay it. Old rusty mess-pork left over from the war and dried-out worm-eaten apples could fetch as much as seventy-five cents a pound. Over at Reardon's Dry Goods Store a good canteen would cost you ten dollars silver. By contrast a whore at the Little Fanny went for a dollar.

I didn't know what in hell I was doing there.

I was making decent money with my dispatches on the reconstruction and the occasional gold-dust yarn to the New York *Sun* but it wasn't the steady income I'd had during the War — when the byline Marion Bell appeared in the paper on a weekly or bi-weekly basis. The money from my father's estate in Massachusetts was not going to last forever. At Gable's Ferry prices I was drinking that up at an alarming rate. Trying to forget what I'd seen in Mexico City more than anything else I imagine.

My paper awhile back had run a cartoon of General Winfield *Old Fuss 'n Feathers* Scott in full ceremonial uniform holding a sword above his head and perched atop a pile of human skulls. That about said it all.

Playing five-card draw that night were Hart, an old German miner named Heilberger and George Donaldson. I barely knew Heilberger but rumor had it that Donaldson was a horse-thief and a card-cheat and the night would bear out at least the last of these rumors.

I was sitting behind Hart slightly off to the right so I could see his cards but he didn't seem to mind. In his left hand he held a short leather thong with one die studding either end and these dice he would pass through his fingers knuckle to knuckle and over and under one another in a smooth fluid motion the trick to which I could not immediately fathom. It may be that whiskey had something to do with this. I was on my fifth and what I thought might be my last glass of the evening but I wasn't making any promises to myself either.

The bet was to Heilberger but he folded so that left Hart and Donaldson.

I don't know how much was on the table but it was a lot. The Little Fanny was crowded that night with Irish and German miners mostly plus the local entrepreneur here and there and the whores of course and when Donaldson bet thirty one of the miners whistled low but loud enough so that you could hear it over Sam Perkins' drunken fiddle-playing.

While Hart was thinking it over Donaldson rolled himself a cigarette and drew the sack shut with the string held between his teeth and when he raised the match there it was, a jack of diamonds staring out at us between his ratty shirt and wool jacket. I saw it and Hart saw it and probably so did Heilberger. I guess that like me Hart simply couldn't believe what he was seeing.

"Jesus and Mary on a broomstick," he said. "You could at least be a little careful, couldn't you?"

He didn't seem angry only more or less annoyed with Donaldson but he drew his gun out nevertheless — some huge grey antique of god knows what vintage — and set it on the table and when Donaldson saw this monstrosity pointed in his direction he began fumbling for his own gun and Hart said *don't do that* which stopped him for a moment but then he went back to fumbling again, just some fool in a panic and Hart said dammit, George, don't *do* that now but by then Donaldson had his own gun out so Hart had no choice but to pull the trigger.

You expected a lot from a gun that big and people were already moving away from behind Donaldson but all we heard was a click.

"Aw shit," said Hart, "that goddamn firing pin."

And Donaldson's face went from white to smiling. It was not a nice smile and it was certainly my turn to move away out of the line of fire but damned if I could. I sat frozen in my chair watching Hart roll the dice between his fingers and over and under his knuckles like he was still considering his card-hand and nothing more and Donaldson fired. And for a split second nothing happened then either.

Then the thing exploded on him. Threw him over and off his chair.

So that he lay writhing and groaning on the rough plank floor with his shirt on fire and a badly scorched face and gunhand until Jess Ake, the barman, threw a bucket of water on him.

That was the gunfight at the Little Fanny Saloon.

We waved away the powder-smoke, Hart and Heilberger and I, and Hart collected his winnings off the table.

"I bet he got that gun up at Gusdorf's," he said. "That man ought to be arrested."

I was amazed at his utter calm. My own stomach was churning whiskey and bile in equal portions — and I hadn't been the fellow staring down a pistol but merely sitting behind somebody who was.

I guessed Hart to be in his late forties, early fifties though it was hard to say and wondered not for the first time what sort of forces had shaped men like some of them you found out here.

If they weren't just plain-out demented, like E.M. "Choctau" Kelly, who was quietly carving a tombstone for Miss Nellie Russell, one of Ginny Smalls' whores over at the Fairview, then the best of them seemed to hold some mix of craziness and courage that served them as a kind of lucky charm.

I think of Old Bill Cooney, who found a black bear snuffling through his ten-dollar sack of coffee beans one morning and got so mad that he chased the bear over half a mile in his stocking feet with nothing in hand should the creature have turned on him but a bottle of lemon beer and a shaving brush.

How could Hart have guessed this outcome?

The answer was he couldn't. It was simply his nature, I suppose, to wait and see. A kind of fatalist patience and presence of mind I couldn't begin to imagine.

We watched as four of the miners took Donaldson by the arms and legs and hauled him outside to what destination I couldn't be certain. Doc Swinlon was surely drunk by this hour but we did have a dentist and a veterinarian who were somewhat less likely to be so. Hart glanced in my direction.

"You look like you're going to be sick, friend," he said.

"I think you're right," I said.

"Get you outside."

He helped me to my feet and out the door to the street with barely a second to lose.

"You shouldn't drink, Bell. You know that?"

"I know."

"Then why do you? I see you every night in there."

"I guess that means you're there pretty much every night too, doesn't it."

Only a drunk would have spoken to him like that but drunk was what I was.

"I can handle it," he said. "You can't." Then he shrugged. "Hell, never mind. It's none of my business. Just thought maybe you might maybe have something better to do."

"I'm no damn prospector, Hart," I said.

And there I was, speaking up to him again. I guess some part of me was offended at the criticism. I should have been amazed he even noticed me among the others let alone knew my name. Also grateful that he'd helped me out of there. I've observed that drunks don't tend toward gratitude.

"So? Neither am I," he said.

He started to walk away.

"Dammit, Hart!"

"What."

I didn't *know* what. I only knew I wanted to stop him. Me, Marion Bell, staggering on a still-whirling street. He looked at me like he was inspecting a mongrel dog who might or might not be useful to him.

"You got a horse, Bell?"

I rented an old bay from Swenson's livery at the going monthly rate.

"'Course I do."

"You want to do something useful for a change, then?"

"I dunno. What'd you have in mind?"

"Let's get you saddled up. We can talk along the way."

✝   ✝

16

Half an hour later we were passing through a campground on the southern edge of town, lanterns glowing in a few of the tents but most of them dark, someone singing a tuneless drunken version of *Annie Laurie* and from the same tent, a whore squealing. As yet Hart hadn't said a thing. He had the thong wrapped around his middle left finger and kept clicking the dice back and forth together and by then I'd sobered up to the extent that at some point I was able to realize that the rythm of the dice was the rythm of his horse's gait.

He waited until we'd passed through the tents and then rolled and lit a cigarette and talked to me.

"You familiar with a gentleman calls himself Mother Knuckles?"

"Big fella?"

"*Big?* You have a gift for understatement, Bell."

"I know him."

"You ever give him a reason to dislike you any?"

"We never met."

"That's good. Because you're going to. I do a little mustanging with Mother now and then. Lots of good horses out here left over from the war which is mostly what we're after. Your real mustang's bred from the old spanish and these belonged to us not long ago but they're still wilder than hell. Maybe if you're very nice to him he'll let you help us out some."

"I never did any mustanging."

"All you got to do is ride for now. We'll handle the rest. You can ride, can't you?"

I wasn't going to dignify that by giving it an answer. I doubt he expected me to.

"What is it you *did* do, Bell? If you don't mind my asking."

"I was a war correspondant for the New York *Sun*. Followed Win Scott's troops into Mexico City."

He nodded. I couldn't say if he was impressed by the fact that I was a writer or bored with the notion or what.

"Scott," he said. "*That* dry tit."

And that was all I had from him until we reached the cabin.

THREE

She said that it was sunset before they'd crossed the plains and reached the river.

She'd ridden all that way with her hands tied behind her back, perched high on the saddle in front of the tall wiry Indio whose name was Gustavo and many times over the journey she felt his prick harden up against her. He had already had both her and Celine but she guessed he wanted more.

She wondered if her sister was experiencing the same in front of Fredo, the fat one with the prickly mustache.

She was sore just about everywhere but especially against the saddle and very thirsty. As they crossed the shallows into Mexico she stayed alert for some means of escape — their horse missing its footing perhaps — but there were none. The Anglo riding point knew his river well. The crossing was smooth and steady.

When the fourth rider leading the pack horse from the back of which over a dozen chickens dangled reached the other side of the river Gustavo turned and said, *Mexico. Is home, no? Why your people leave here?*

She felt no wish to answer him.

"I see your eyes, little one," he said. "I see the way you fight. You and the sisters, I think you are the same."

She found it hard to believe that a foul-smelling dog like this had sisters of any kind so she asked him.

"What sisters?"

"*Las hermanas de lupo. Las hermanas* del diablo. As old as the mountains, little one. As old as the gods are old. Just like you."

He laughed.

"You know," he said, "I think maybe they will have to kill you."

†   †

The night was moonless and starless beneath low-lying clouds and she saw the bonfires well before the settlement. There were four fires and as many wooden outbuildings on either side of an old hacienda which had seen better days and as they approached she was surprised and puzzled at how many people these mostly small buildings must have housed within, some of them *soldados* like the ones they rode with but most of them women, young and dirty and moving listlessly at their various chores, hauling water and wood and cooking and stoking the flames.

Even before the old crone stepped out of nowhere out of the smoke in front of them she knew there was something very wrong here because many of these women were Anglos — fragile-looking blonde women working side by side with Mexican peasant girls and she thought she already knew how this collection had come to be. Some of them wore little more than rags and some what appeared to be castoff dance-hall costumes badly torn and wore grotesque amounts of makeup on their bruised filthy faces perhaps to shame them and some were clearly ill and staggered under the burden of their toil. She heard moans and laughter and from somewhere a muffled scream.

Then the old *hechicera* stepped out of the smoke billowing around them and her fears for their safety in this place turned to something more akin to dread.

As old as the hills? No, she thought. But old enough. Unknowably old.

Beneath the black concentric circles painted across her cheeks and chin and the black crescent moons which hollowed the eyes burning up at them and the black slashings across the lips and nose, her skin hung off her face like slugs crawling. She wore some kind of thin gown, ragged and nearly transparent so it was possible to see her withered layered flesh beneath and the dugs with their huge dark nipples pointed down toward the earth. Her hair was long and matted and she smelled of brimstone and rotted blood. On her head was the sunbleached hollowed-out skull of a coyote, its top row of teeth still intact.

The coyote's grin seemed to match her own.

In each of her hands she held a living rattlesnake gripped below the heads which twisted writhing around her arms. At the sight of these or perhaps the smell of her the horses shied and whinnied and tried to move away.

Gustavo removed his hat to her. The Anglo Ryan merely nodded as they passed.

Still amazed by this apparition Elena turned in the saddle and saw two younger women step up beside her, these both middle-aged she thought, each dressed in black. One was bone-thin and hard-looking, grim and expressionless, clean and neat. The other stocky, with cruel peasant's features.

She had just met the Valenzura sisters. Old Eva, Maria, and Lucia.

Her guardians in hell.

FOUR

"WHAT THE GODDAMN KIND OF FIRST-THING-IN-THE-MORNING HORSESHIT IS THIS?"

The calfskins layered across the cabin's floor had seemed sufficiently large for three the night before but now seemed much too small for two. I awoke to the bellowing of a huge bearded bear of a man in sweatstained longjohns staring at my feet directly across from his balding head. What had been merely an admittedly large yet gently snoring figure in the dark was now the red-eyed face of hostility. It seemed likely as not that he would reach over and tear off my feet and beat me with them.

Where was Hart when I needed him?

Then I smelled the coffee.

"Easy, Mother. The gentleman's name is Marion T. Bell."

He was standing at a scorched blackened stove which might well have dated back to the War of 1812.

"Bell? I never hearda no goddamn Bell!"

He got up and stepped into a pair of frayed grey trousers and pulled up the suspenders and that was that, he was dressed. I couldn't remember for the life of me where I'd

23

put my own and didn't want to move just yet. Not until he'd settled down some. I watched him stomp across the floor to Hart and Hart pour something steaming brown and nearly as thick as syrup out of a stained tin pan.

He divided the stuff evenly into three tin cups and handed one to Mother who drank it straight away.

It was possible to imagine at that moment that his lunch might be a Joshua Tree burst aflame.

"Thought we could use a third hand."

"Him? Christ on a cross, Hart. He's *green*. Look at him!"

He turned to me. I was up and searching for my shirt and pants. I found them easily enough, neatly folded on the only chair in the room, my boots beneath the chair. Hart's doing.

"Yer *green*, ain't ya! Jesus Christ, Hart. You throw this dumb green kid at me first thing in the goddamn morning and I dunno what to think, I really don't. I dunno what the hell's on your mind sometimes. You know that? God damned if I do. 'Spose we could use a third body out there, though. Yeah, I guess we could. Can he ride? He can ride, can't he? *Can you* ride*, goddammit?*"

"He rode with Scott into Mexico City."

"Win Scott? *That* dry tit? Well what the hell. I'm Mother Knuckles you're Marion T. Bell. Pleased to meet ya."

He put out his hand.

It was a handshake I will not readily forget.

† †

It was not my own horse but a young sorrel they had me on that day and I won't forget her either, because while I knew nothing of the nature of our undertaking she knew

24

everything. We found five horses grazing in an arroyo, beautiful creatures, chestnut and bay — not at all like the tough unlovely beasts descended from the spanish breed but tall and strong — and we herded them stricken with some primal fear of us yelping riders through a long wide wash directly into the box canyon I learned that Hart and Mother had used many times before, Mother working left and Hart working right and the horse Suzie and I center, the easiest position to hold because the wild horses would naturally want to break to either side.

Suzie did the work and all I had to do was hold on — a daunting enough proposition in itself with her darting left and right according to the horses' movements ahead of her, riding at a far faster speed than any I'd ever had need of before and then once we'd trapped them, riding back and forth across the mouth of the canyon turning on a dime to discourage three of them from bolting for freedom while Hart and Mother choke-roped the other two to the ground, looping and tying off the ropes around the forelegs first and then the back, returning to their horses to repeat the process with two of the three chestnuts until finally Mother took the fifth and last alone.

For a man the size of Mother it was amazing to watch him work with such sheer dexterity and speed. You more or less expected it of Hart. But Mother was a revelation. The power in him was clear. The grace was not. Yet it was there in full measure.

As the weeks went by it was he and not Hart who showed me how to tie a slip knot, how to throw a rope, why and for how long to force a hard-ridden mount to wait before food and water, wiping the sweat off her ribs and backbone and brushing her down until she cooled some. Hart had a distance about him. Mother nearly lived up to his name.

I can't say I ever became expert at what we did. But with Mother's help I didn't tend to make a fool of myself either. Hart and I still delivered our custom to the Little Fanny many evenings — occasionally Mother too — but with a morning's work ahead of us my habits moderated considerably. You didn't want to be riding Suzie with a pounding headache. I had money in my pockets and it more or less tended to stay there. There were nights I simply remained home at the cabin and wrote instead. My dispatches to New York increased proportionally.

So while it was Mother who taught me, it was Hart I had to thank for turning me around in the first place. And because of that, his reserve never bothered me. I figured it was just his way.

That changed when we met Elena.

Then he began to worry me.

FIVE

"You, writer," she said. *"Take this down.
"They will find it on our bodies."*
So I did.

SIX

We did well some days and other days saw nothing for our troubles but empty waterskins and dust between our teeth and on this particular evening with dark fast approaching all we had as we rode through the scrub were two squat mustangs hobbled behind us. We'd come very far afield and you could hear the river behind us over the *click, click, click* of Hart's dice.

Mother was riding back aways with the mustangs and gnawing some dried beef he'd fished out of his saddlebag. There'd been the usual silence between Hart and I but this time I'd resolved to break it. I'd been pondering something awhile.

"The night you brought me out here, Hart," I said, "in the bar with Donaldson. Donaldson was ready to shoot you. You just sat there."

"So? What's your point?"

"So, he was ready to *shoot* you. It was the damnedest thing I ever saw."

"I guess he would have, wouldn't he."

"Hart, you looked so calm about it!"

"Guess I was. Pretty calm anyways. I'm not a real imaginative man, Bell. Most things, I walk in prepared as best I can. Then I trust to luck, that's all."

I had to wonder if part of my problem being here instead of back in Boston or Cambridge or New York was that I *was* an imaginative man. I could and did imagine rattlesnakes under the bed and scorpions in my boots and I poked beneath the bed with a stick and shook out my boots with due diligence every morning. There were a thousand ways to die out here and I'd seen many of them first hand in Puebla, Churubusco and Mexico City during the war. It didn't take much to imagine my own death courting me.

The west was not NELLIE, THE RAGPICKER'S DAUGHTER or even THE ADVENTURES OF PECOS BILL. No penny dreadful. The west was gangrene and thirst and rivers red with blood and skies so big they could crush you like a bug.

"You got family, Bell?" he said. "Never did ask you."

"Brother. Couple of nephews by now I think. Never do write one another. Why?"

He didn't really answer, only nodded.

"It's a good thing, family," he said.

† † †

We were passing some low thick scrub off left and suddenly the horses began to shy. Hart pulled his own mare to a halt and sat listening. I followed suit with Suzie. Mother rode up slow behind us.

"What we got here, John?" he said.

"Something in there. Could be a cat, maybe."

Hart pulled his Winchester out of its scabbard, cocked it and lay it across his saddle and we could hear something in there all right, moving in our direction not twenty feet away. We sat and listened and then Hart swung down abruptly off his saddle saying *that's no damn cat* and Mother and I heard it too then, a moan and labored breathing and as Hart stepped toward the brush his rifle at the ready they stumbled out practically into him. Two dark shapes one trying to support the other and failing, both going down to the earth in front of him.

I saw him step back reflexively and then for the first time I clearly saw the two women. In what little light we had it was hard to say whether it was dirt or blood that covered them but they both were naked — that we saw right away.

I swung off my horse and so did Mother.

"*Damn!*" he said.

Close up you could see that one of them was just a girl not more than sixteen, a pale slim redhead, her face pale and bloody and awash with pain, her breath coming in deep stuccato gulps if and when it came at all.

The other scared hell out of me.

The look of her was savage.

There was no other word for it. She looked up at us on her knees holding onto the Anglo girl and she was at once beautiful and terrifying — something in her eyes cold and bright as a snake's eyes or fierce as a wolf with its leg long caught in a trap and you could see the Indio blood in her broad high cheekbones but it was far more than that, something older and far more primitive. In the look of her you could almost see another world entirely.

I saw Hart flinch as her eyes went up to him and could barely believe that anything could make him do so and then saw what was perhaps the source of this woman's ferocity.

Her face had been slashed with a knife from cheek to chin. She wore the mark of the bullwhip across her back and thighs. On her left inner thigh I could make out the letter V branded into her and nearly healed. Her wrists and ankles were lacerated as though she'd been tied repeatedly and for a very long time. The stab-wound in her lower back oozed blood.

And it was she who'd been supporting the Anglo girl.

"Lord in heaven," said Mother.

He went to her and bent down and extended his hand.

"You're all right now," he said. "Take it easy. Easy."

Her eyes left Hart, who had put up his rifle but otherwise hadn't moved — it was as though he wouldn't go anywhere *near* this woman badly wounded though she was but there was no time to wonder about that nor any of his behavior — and went to Mother directly in front of her. Naked and unarmed she still looked dangerous as hell to me and she clutched the girl to her breasts.

Mother glanced at Hart and frowned and then looked at me.

"Gimme a hand here, Bell." And to her he said, "you got to let go of her now, ma'am. You got to let us take her. We'll take good care of her, all right? I promise. We'll take good care of the both you folks."

That *coiled* look in her eyes gradually seemed to soften. She took hold of Mother's hand finally and let the girl fall gently away into my arms and allowed Mother to pick her up which he did as easily as though she were a child. He carried her to his horse and set her down a moment beside it and then unhitched his blanket-roll and wrapped it around her.

I didn't know how to handle my own part of this. The girl seemed so fragile I was afraid that the mere act of holding her might be enough to kill her somehow and I could see the deep knife-wound in her ribcage steadily oozing blood and the vivid gash across her forehead. Finally Hart took the whole thing out of my hands.

"Give her here," he said.

He handed me his rifle and lifted her away.

† †

It took us a good three hours to reach the cabin and by then the moon was full and bright. I'd been bringing up the rear leading the mustangs and the Mexican woman I'd know as Elena rode the horse's back behind Mother, her arms barely encircling his massive waist. The redheaded girl faced Hart in front of him on the saddle and he had one arm across her back pressing her to his chest and keeping her blanket in place around her the other hand holding the reins.

I broke away from them and corraled the mustangs and rode Suzie hard to catch up with them at the cabin. Mother already had Elena seated on the rickety front steps and I saw him reach up and lift the younger girl gently away from Hart and saw that she'd bled out all over the front of him. His shirt and trousers were soaked and gleaming black with her.

Her head lolled back. Her arms dangled. Her face was pale as marble and her eyes were wide and empty. Dark blood had spilled out over her lips and chin.

"Looks like that happened quite a while ago," Mother said.

"It did."

"You should have said something."

"I did," said Hart. "I said goodbye."

He swung off his horse and tethered her and stepped past Elena whose eyes seemed to fault him personally for the girl's death and into the cabin.

† †

33

It was Mother who buried her. Mother who cleaned and bandaged Elena's wounds.

Hart would not go near her.

There was something between these two that was almost as though they knew one another from some point in time previous though when I asked him about it all he did was laugh and I didn't much care for the sound of his laughter either.

By the time Mother was finished with the burying we'd tended to the horses and Elena was asleep, wrapped in blankets yet cold and sweating with fever. It was anybody's guess if she would make it through the night. Mother walked through the doorway and set down the shovel and I handed him a cup of coffee. He walked over to Hart who was arranging logs on the fire.

"Somebody branded her," he said.

"I know. This one too."

"What the hell you make of that?"

"I don't know what to make of it, Mother."

"Me neither. Knife-wound was what killed her, though. That's certain. I had myself a look at it and it was deep. I'm surprised the poor thing managed to stay alive as long as she did."

"The young tend towards living."

Mother sipped his hot coffee and glanced around the cabin.

"How you want to do this?"

"Do what?"

"Where you want to sleep?"

"The floor. Let her have the skins, the fire. Let her sweat it out there. We got enough blankets between us."

Mother looked over at Elena. He looked almost shy.

"I never had a woman in my house," he said. "Not ever."

"You still don't. You got a Mex."

"You figure?"

"Don't you?"

Mother looked at her again.

"No, Hart. Can't say that I do. I was wondering. She by chance remind you of somebody?"

Then it was Hart's turn to look.

"No," he said, "nobody. Not a soul."

His voice was flat and cold as I'd ever heard it.

I thought that lying didn't suit him either.

† †

At first I thought it was the coyotes' lonesome howling that awoke me in the night but it was not. It was Elena, her voice, the coyotes providing only appropriate accompaniment to whatever strange harsh language she was speaking which was not english nor spanish but some tongue I'd never heard before nor ever wished to hear, a violent whisper, a chant almost devoid of long sonorous vowels but which were instead described in a series of short breathy interludes between the explosive dominant consonants that clicked and hissed and barked like something drawn directly from nature, from the wild, from *a jungle*, here where there was no jungle, the rattle and slither of venomous snakes, a hive of bees, the yip of a coyote, the rustle of leaves in dense air, all of these intermingled and which repeated themselves over and over as she knelt rocking back and forth naked on her knees before the fire, sweat rolling down her long scarred back, feeding broken bits of kindling to the flames. Propped up beside her against the logs was a small crucifix made of twigs and bound with strips of cloth. Beside that a tin plate of cornmeal, another of coffee beans and a third containing two broken eggs.

She had raided our supplies silent as a ghost.

And in that flickering light you could believe she *was* some ghost made flesh. Some ancient Indio demon summoning her bretheren.

It was three hundred years since Cortez. *Aztec, Maya, Toltec, Mexica.* All gone. Or were they?

I remembered the wildness in her eyes when first we'd seen her.

I wondered what those eyes held now.

She reached over for the plate of cornmeal and tossed it into the fire. In the woodsmoke I now smelled cornbread. She began to tremble. She set the plate down and reached for the coffee beans and did the same and now I smelled morning coffee. The trembling increased. Her head rolled side to side. The rocking became an up and down motion. Her chanting increased its pace. She reached again.

I wasn't surprised to smell fried eggs as though cooking in a pan.

She slid her legs apart and the sudden erotic charge *did* take me by surprise because in that single movement all I watched and heard clarified and I knew it was some life-force she was summoning there before the fire and I could imagine a man there all along and only this moment revealed beneath her thrusting up silent and invisible as she thrust down.

Something made me turn and steal a glance at Hart and Mother. Mother faced the far wall, asleep.

Hart's eyes were open. He was watching.

She groaned and shuddered and fell silent. Her head dropped forward and then her body so that she rested on all fours for a moment breathing hard and then threw herself to the side and onto her blankets. I closed my eyes and pretended sleep.

Real sleep was long coming.

SEVEN

She told us she remembered the day she felt the full weight of what had happened to them. Not just the rapes and the humiliations, the cramped airless foul-smelling sleeping quarters or the mule work in the yard with the goats or chickens or in the garden under the ferocious blazing sun or in the stifling laundry or kitchen, all of them hobbled like horses. Not just the the bullwhip.

She remembered her first time inside the hacienda.

† †

She has been there merely five days. She has not seen her sister Celine in the last two of those days and that is a torture too. She is drawing a bucket of water from the well. It's needed in the kitchen.

Maria, the middle sister, thin-lipped, harsh and grim is beckoning to her from the porch. Do that later, *she says.* Come here. *Elena sets the bucket down and walks past the blackened remains of one bonfire and then another. She has trouble climbing the steps to the porch. With her ankles tied together she can only take the steps one at a time. Maria is impatient.* Hurry little bitch, *she says.*

On the outside the hacienda is old and shabby. Inside she sees the Valenzuras' wealth. A short corridor leads to a huge room through oak double doors. Gold chandeliers hung from gleaming intricately-worked punched tin ceilings, marble fireplaces, armoires and shelves and side towers carved from juniper, oak and mohagany, painted standing bookshelves, yarn paintings and bark paintings of monkeys, snakes and lizards, gold sun masks and jaguar masks, immense gilt mirrors. And everywhere the image of the wolf.

In iron statuary, in fired clay, in stone. In paint and embroidery.

The wolf is their nahaul. *The animal to which they link their destiny.*

She follows Maria through the vast room which holds these treasures past a polished oak staircase which separates two corridors, one brightly lit and lushly carpeted with paintings on the walls and potted cacti blooming reds and yellows, the other shabby, dark and bare. Their destination is through this latter corridor and already she is disturbed at what she hears. They walk past six small rooms from which the doors have been removed, set staggered to each other, three on either side. The first is empty but for a single bed, its mattress dark with stains. In the second a young Mexican girl wearing only a rebozo draped across her shoulders huddles weeping in a corner. Her wrists are shackled together in front of her.

The third is empty too but for a cobweb maze of heavy chains which depend from the ceiling. Directly across from it the fourth room is similar but inhabited. A woman of about Elena's age hangs swaying from from a pair of manacles in the center of the room. The woman appears to be unconcious, possibly dead. Her filthy serape has been torn through down the middle. Her feet are mere inches off the floor and her face is bloody from recent beating.

At the fifth door Maria nearly collides with a fat Mexican soldado *who is emerging from the room, tucking his shirt into his pants. He meekly nods and steps hastily aside for her. As she passes Elena glances into the room and sees a young woman with bright red tangled hair sobbing naked sprawled across the bed.*

The worst by far is the sixth room. She has been listening to the sounds coming from here since they entered the corridor.

Someone is being horribly beaten.

And here she sees men she knows — Gustavo, the flat-faced Indio halfbreed who brought her to this place and Fredo, the fat one who rode with her sister. Fredo holds a short studded whip. They stand on either side of a table. Tied spread-eagled to the legs of the table face-up across it is a young girl of exactly Celine's coloring and build and Elena stops dead in her tracks sure at first that it is *Celine, absolutely certain of it and in her rage and fear at the bloody carnage in front of her nearly vaults into the room despite her hobbled legs, the threat of death itself won't stop her, until the girl turns her head and she sees by the livid kidney-shaped birthmark on her neck that it is not Celine after all but someone else's sister fated to endure this.*

Come on, *says Maria.* Whore.

She follows her with difficulty, the hobbles chafing at her ankles, up a back set of stairs which were probably once for the servants' use and into a second corridor. The sounds she is hearing now are not precisely screams but they are sounds of great distress and they are female. Maria waits ahead of her at the entrance to the first door she comes to and angrily beckons her in and now she hears also the unmistakable crying of a baby. Elena follows her in.

The room is lit with more than a dozen scented candles. They do not quite mask the scent of raw flesh and unclean sweat and urine which eminates from the woman upon the bed. The woman has just given birth and the old hag Eva holds it crying in her arms. It is wrapped in a thin white towel. With Eva grinning toothlessly down at it, she thinks, anyone would cry. The pig-faced sister Lucia is cleaning up the afterbirth. Behind them Paddy Ryan stands in shadow.

Male or female? *Maria asks.*

Lucia shrugs. Male, *she says.*

As Eva predicted, *Maria says.* Too bad.

She turns to Elena. Take it, *she says. Elena has no wish to come anywhere near this flithy creature or this child but she does as she's told and manages to do so without touching the old woman's clawed yellow hands.* Are you ready, Ryan? *Maria says.*

I am, *he says.*

She turns to Elena again. Go with Mr. Ryan.

Ryan leads her back the way she's come and she refuses to gaze into any of the rooms now despite the young girl's screaming and the crack of the whip. The baby's crying is constant and it seems she can do nothing to stop it. He leads her across the courtyard to the barren wasted hill beyond and they begin to climb. She has never been up this hill before but she knows what they call it — Garanta del Diablo *— the Devil's Mouth. She has seen the black plumes of smoke which drift continually on the wind.*

As they near the top she stops to catch her breath and glances back toward the hacienda. All three sisters are on the porch, watching them. The baby has at last stopped crying. Ryan has disappeared from sight atop the plateau. The sun beats down. She continues on.

At the top she sees him waiting for her standing beside a wall-like pyramid of blackened skulls. The wall is tall as he is.

The air is thick with tarry smoke wafting up from behind him.

Some of the skulls are very small but all of them are human.

She begins to cry.

Bring it here.

You can't do this! *she says.*

His voice is quiet and without passion. When he smiles the scar on his cheek contracts . Sure I can. Bring it here. Else you both go. Up to you.

It's a child!

A boy's no use to us here. That's just the way it is. *He draws his sidearm and spins the chamber.* Your choice, he says.

She walks over until she's close enough to gaze into the pit maybe six or seven feet across and sees the fire burning a sullen red and blue within, sees the long-handled iron scoop which lies beside it and closes her eyes as Ryan takes the baby from her arms and hears it begin to cry again perhaps from the loss of her and she is crying too as he tells her she can go back to her work now and she is halfway down the hill moving slowly when the baby's crying stops abruptly and all she hears is wind in the hills and the bleating of the goats in the yard.

Her own tears linger off and on all day long — she feels as though she has lost her own child or a brother — and only stop when lying in her bunk late at night she peers through the weathered wooden slats of the wall to their sleeping quarters and sees Celine with a group of others throwing sand over one of the bonfires, her little sister looking tired and bruised and beaten. But alive.

EIGHT

"Get up, Bell. She's gone, goddammit!"

It was Mother, storming into the cabin.

"What? What's going on?"

"She took my horse, goddammit. She took the goddamn roan."

"How...?"

"My horse and Hart's Winchester. Gear and saddle too."

He kicked her blankets off into a corner.

"The girl did?"

"Jesus, Bell. Who the hell do you think I'm talking about? The Mex! The goddamn woman!"

I couldn't believe she'd have the strength to saddle a horse and ride. Not the way she was wounded. Then I remembered what I'd seen last night.

"Where's Hart?"

"Outside. If I were you I'd check my clothes, see what's missing. You're the smallest and I doubt she rode outa here naked. I liked that horse, goddammit."

He was right. A shirt and a pair of trousers were missing from my pack. Not the best of what I had but not the worst either. It was nothing compared to Mother's horse or Hart's rifle but enough so that I felt somewhat betrayed by her too. If she'd asked I'd have given them freely. But she hadn't.

Hart was sitting on the porch in his boots and longjohns, smoking a cigarette and twirling his dice. I sat down next to him with a cup of coffee looking out into the corral at the two new restless mustangs there. The day was already hot and clear. I sipped the coffee and considered.

"Last night, Hart? By the fire?"

"Yes. What about it?

"Hell, I don't know. I don't know what to say. It was pretty damn amazing, wouldn't you say? She was..."

"She was healing, Bell. Healing the old way. How'd you like it?"

"All things told? I didn't. Truth is she scared me."

He smiled but there wasn't any humor in it.

"You've got good instincts, son. You ever have serious dealings with a Mex, you hold on tight to those instincts."

He got up and tossed away the cigarette and turned toward the cabin.

"So what're we gonna do?"

He stopped and seemed to ponder that a moment.

"Well, Mother's got other horses but I haven't got another Winchester. So I guess we go on after her."

I considered telling him he could have mine. That's how much I liked the prospect of this enterprise. But I didn't.

✝   ✝

We trailed her all morning and into the afternoon, past flowering yucca and greasewood, prickly pear and tall saguaro, through scrub thick and thin and over grass and owl's clover. We saw a pair of jackrabbits in full rut and hawks riding the thermals high above. In the mostly dry dusty terrain her tracks were clear. To Mother and Hart if not to me.

You want to tell me what the hell she's doing? Mother said.

Mother, you know *what she's doing,* Hart said. *Going right back to where she came from.*

It was late afternoon before we found her lying beneath a gnarled clump of trees propped up against one of them, the roan tethered beside her and Hart's Winchester lying across her lap. She looked bad, exhausted — nearly as bad as when first we first saw her — and some of her wounds had begun bleeding again beneath my shirt and Mother's dressings. She said nothing when we reined in and only glared at Hart and watched him as he dismounted his blaze-face black and walked over and took his rifle, walked back to the horse and shoved it in its scabbard and then returned and bent down to her suddenly and took her cheeks between his fingers and squeezed.

She was cut deep there and it must have hurt like hell but she said nothing.

"You want to remember something, woman," he said. "Your little friend died all over me last night. That matter to you? Do you give a good goddamn about that? I don't think you do. This what we get for helping you?"

He squeezed harder. Blood seeped through the bandage beneath his thumb.

"Hey, Hart," I said. "Jesus, Hart!"

She was a thief but she was hurt and a woman and I was nearly down off Suzi when Mother reached over and stopped me.

"Leave it be, son."

"You do that, Bell," he said, and then to her, "now are you going to talk to me? Because I'm a little tired of you looking at me in Apache, if you get my meaning. You stole from me and you stole from Mother and Bell over there and I want to know why and if you *don't* start talking to me soon I may just take the roan and leave you under this goddamn shade-tree for the wolves and coyotes this evening. Because I am looking at one damn fool here, doing what you're doing."

He released her and stood away. Finally she nodded.

"Can I have a drink of water?" she said. The first words in english we'd heard out of her.

"Hell," said Mother, "you can have *dinner*. We all will. Then we'll talk. That okay with you, Hart?"

"That's fine, Mother."

Now what's your goddamn name? he said and she told him.

✝   ✝

We got her on the horse and rode in the rapid-falling sunset to a creek we knew of where the mustangs liked to take their water evenings. She told us she wanted a bath, that it would make her feel much better and nobody tried to talk her out of it. Hart said he'd come along. The horses needed watering he said and our canteens needed filling. It didn't seem quite proper to me but nobody tried to talk him out of it either. Not even her. I could only figure she wasn't much for privacy.

Mother had thought to bring along fresh bandages so replacing them after her bath wasn't going to be a problem.

We watched them descend the slope to the stream, Hart leading our horses and Elena the one she'd stolen from Mother and then we set about gathering what firewood the meager scrub around us had to offer.

"What's his problem, Mother?" I asked when we were nearly through.

46

"Who? Hart? You mean with the Mex?"

I nodded.

"Hell, Hart knows the Mex well. Most of 'em are still half Indian you understand. So you got to show 'em your *cojones*. Get them to respect you. Otherwise they're liable to slit your throat one night just because they like the shine of your boots. You know that Hart was a drover during Win Scott's Puebla campaign."

I said I hadn't. I was surprised to hear it in fact and told him so — that I was with Scott myself and Hart knew that and so did he. So why hadn't they told me?

"Hell, I was there too," Mother said. "I never told you, neither."

"Why?"

"You never asked, Bell. Anyhow that was where we met, Hart and me. Summer of '47, just after Santa Anna got his ass handed to him at Cerro Gordo, just before the push to Mexico City."

"You were garrisoned there? In Puebla?"

"Nope. Supply train. Hell of a time for everybody, though, no matter where you were."

"I know. You had Santa Anna on the one hand scurrying around scrounging for troops and cash and us just sitting there waiting for reinforcement and filling up the goddamn hospitals. For months in that garrison we lost twelve or so men every day to heat and dysentery and all you could do was wrap them in the shit-stained blankets they died in and dump them into those pits they had outside there. Some dazzling military mind, that Scott had. Bastard never stopped drilling those boys though they were lucky to get half rations. And there he is, waiting for the 9th New England Regiment I think it was to come fill his goddamn ranks while he decimates them on the parade grounds. Crazy sonovabitch."

47

"You never saw the worst of it, though, Bell."

"I saw Mexico City."

"That was plenty bad, I grant you. But the worst was the guerrillas. I was with a supply train, as I say. Hart was a drover. We saw plenty of those sons of bitches and we saw what they did. First they'd steal you blind and then just kill you for the pleasure of it. Cut a man's heart out and tongue out and rip his pecker off and string 'em from the limb of a tree with his body propped up beneath it. Supposed to scare the hell out of you and believe me, it did."

We had what we judged was enough dry juniper and brush for the fire so we began gathering the stones with which to bank it.

"Care to hear a story? About Hart back then?"

"Sure."

I was as curious about Hart as I'd ever been. He was still a mystery to me. I knew a little about Mother. He'd come from Missouri, never married and his father was a Presbyterian preacher of Scots-Irish ancestry — long dead from the bottle. His sister and two brothers remained back east. All Hart would say was he'd been around here and there. On Hart any light shed was welcome.

"Well, this was a couple months before we met and I heard about it a while before then.

"Hart's herding cattle and a wagon full of salt beef and hardtack through an arroyo, few miles north of Puebla. He's hired on for three dollars a day, pretty good money, right? The leader's a fella named Charles Berry — he was the one that told me all about this so you got to know it's not some made-up story — fella from Rhode Island, of an entrepreneurial nature you might say, who figures to make himself a tidy bit of money courtesy of the U.S. Cavalry. There's two other drovers beside Hart and fifty head of beef.

"So this Mex rides down into the arroyo. Small fella dressed to beat the band — high boots with big silver spurs, big white sombrero, buckskin breeches, white shirt, red silk sash around his waist, bridle and saddle both covered with studded silver — and he rides up smiling on this fine chestnut stallion and Berry's thinking, can't be no trouble here, this Mex has got landowner written all over him. So he pulls up the wagon and they commence to chattin'.

"Hart's working the cattle and watching and pretty soon he sees that the Mex ain't smiling any more and he's pointing up the arroyo. He sees Berry look in that direction so he looks too and sure enough, there are seven or eight men up there pointing army-issue carbines down at them. They talk a little more but not so casual this time and Berry gets down off the wagon and strolls on over.

"'Boys,' he says, 'they're taking our goods and cattle and I don't see how we can stop 'em. What we're going to do now I guess is just ride off a ways and that means we get to keep on living. Hart, I'll ride with you.' Hart gives him a hand up onto his horse and off they go — and Berry's feeling lucky to still have a tongue and a pecker on him, never mind the beef.

"When it gets toward evening they're oh, maybe half a mile away. Country's like this is here, half prairie, half scrub. They find water for the horses and settle in for the night, figuring to make Puebla by early afternoon. And then Hart comes up with his proposal.

"He's been thinking it over he says and if Berry will part with fifteen dollars over his three dollar a day salary he'll bring him back his herd and the wagonload of salt beef and hardtack to boot. All they've got to do is stay where they are for three, maybe four nights. Just stay put and wait on him. Well sure, says Berry. So Hart borrows a double-barrel shotgun from one of the other drovers, loads it with sixteen buckshot, saddles his horse and rides back the way they come."

We arranged the rocks in a tight wide circle and Mother adjusted them to his liking and then started piling on the tinder and wood inside.

"It's after midnight by the time he finds the herd. They're settled down into a clearing. Now, Hart's been riding this herd a good two weeks by then so the cattle know him, they're used to him, and they don't make a fuss about him being there. So he just lays down amongst 'em. Lays right down in the middle of the herd facing the stars with the shotgun across his chest. He waits and the cattle mill around some.

"And pretty soon one of the Mex herders rides in close enough and Hart lets him have a barrel and that's the end of the herder. The cattle start moving, naturally. They're stomping and snorting and jumpy as hell what with the shotgun blast and the gunpowder and the smell of blood and Hart can feel stampede in the air but it ain't happened yet.

"So a second herder comes riding toward the shot, cursing his buddy and no doubt wondering what in the hell would make him do a damn fool thing like firing off a round in the middle of a herd of beef and Hart stands up and gives him the second barrel, blows him right out of his saddle. Then moves off into the brush opposite their campsite.

"'Cause then of course there *is* a stampede. And while the Mex are all running around and chasin' their ponies and saddling 'em and then runnin' them into a lather trying to stop the damn thing Hart just punches his blanket roll into a likely-enough pillow and lies down to get some sleep.

"Next night, same thing.

"Except this time the second rider's wise to him once he's shot the first. So Hart has to hunt him down through a mess of half-crazed pissed off cattle disturbed by gunfire two goddamn nights in a row. Hart gets him, though.

"Third night he can only manage to kill the first one but that's just fine because now they're down to three riders from the original eight and they haven't gotten far with all the roundup work they been doing, they're pretty dispirited, so the next afternoon Hart says the hell with it and they're rolling down a wash when he catches up to them, shotgun cradled in his arm and tells the Mex driving the wagon that he's the one who shot his buddies and that he can either give up the cattle and the wagon or they can have it out right then and there.

"Next day he rides back to where Berry and the others are waiting with all but four head of cattle. Berry said in all truth he had to give it to the Mex — they were nasty little sons of bitches but they were pretty good herders to come out of three stampedes with only four head unaccounted for. By then Hart's bushed, so Berry sends the other two boys back for the supply wagon and they find it right where Hart said he'd left it though there was nothing to stop the Mex from taking that at least.

"'Cept of course the worry that Hart might come after 'em again."

Hell of a story, I thought. Were it not Hart he was talking about but some other man unknown to me I'd have written it up as soon as I got to pen and paper. But I didn't think he'd care to be the subject of a story in a New York daily.

"That doesn't explain it, though," I said.

"Explain what?"

"The way he treats her. His problems with the Mex."

"Mex killed his stepbrother at Churubusco. Kid about your age, had he lived."

I saw Hart leading the horses up from the stream. Elena's horse among them. She wasn't with them. In his free hand he twirled the dice.

"I never did meet a man who loved his dice so."

Mother laughed and set a match to the kindling. "Hell, those belonged to his wife. Dealer in a saloon over in San Antonio, time they met. Tough, handsome woman, she was. Spirited I suppose you'd say. A little like this one here, only white. Ran off with a fella whose game was blackjack I believe."

Interesting, I thought. I'd learned more about Hart in a single conversation than I had in the past two months. Information about him was coming at me thick and fast and the thought occured to me that it was as though somehow Elena was the catalyst for all that. Elena and whatever it was she was up to.

"I'd never have thought of him as married," I said.

"He *ain't* married, son. Not no more. 'Cept maybe to me."

I watched him pass us by and nod and tether the four horses and wondered if he knew we'd been talking about him from the silence between us and if he'd care one way or another. I was reaching for a piece of mesquite in the pile behind us when he walked over.

"I think you want to leave that," he said.

"Huh?"

"Back off a little."

I stood and took a step back and Hart kicked at the pile and I heard the snake's sharp rattle before I saw the thing coiling itself into a tight deadly ball, its attention moving from Hart to me directly in front of it just as Hart's boot came down squarely on its head.

"Jesus *Christ,* Hart!"

"Saw it crawl in there just now. You want to be more careful, Bell."

"You just *stepped* on the damn thing. They *bite* for chrissake!"

"Not if you step on them first, they don't."

It had easily been within striking distance of me. I was shaken. A snakebite wasn't normally a fatal thing if you got to it right away but you never knew and you wouldn't want to try your luck.

"Hell, Hart. Don't you *like* life?"

"No more than that snake did, probably. But then I don't dislike it either."

I turned and saw Elena coming up the embankment. Her clothes were wet and her hair was wet and she looked refreshed and younger and very lovely. Mother smiled.

"Hand me that rattlesnake, Bell," he said. "Mr. Hart just supplemented our rations. It's time for dinner."

†   †

The snake was tasty spitted over the fire and went nicely with the beans, salt beef and hardtack. By the time she was finished eating I thought Elena looked stronger. I was amazed at her powers of recovery. Her long hair gleamed in the firelight. I mopped my plate with the last of the bread and gathered up the others' to take to the river. Hart stopped me.

"Time we talked," he said.

He looked at Elena and I sat back down again and waited. Hart opened the whiskey beside him and we passed it around. Elena waved it away.

She drank some water from the canteen instead and told her story.

†　　†

I knew full well that shortly after the war large parts of Mexico had become colonized by hundreds of white settlers attracted to the land, the cheap living and the notion of life as conquerors. I also knew that conquerors did not tend to be generous with the conquered. Especially the brand of soldier who'd campaigned in Mexico.

If he was regular army he'd probably already fought in the Indian wars at one time or another in the very recent past and to him a Mexican was just another half-caste Apache. Rape had been common during the wars on both sides and some men — far too many men — had developed a taste for it, for violence and a woman who'd let him do whatever he damn well felt like because she knew she needed to just to stay alive.

It was a taste they brought with them across the border into Mexico.

There was money in their pockets.

They could pay for what they wanted.

There was a market among their number growing fast as weeds in a graveyard and the Valenzuras supplied that market.

Elena, her sister Celine and the young woman whose name she never knew had tried to flee their fate there.

She had cut away their hobbles with a dull kitchen knife sharpened over time while the others slept and secreted in her skirt and they'd hidden in some scrub behind and below the hill she called Garanta del Diablo until darkness fell and then had tried their run. They got as far as the river.

"I pulled one of them off the Anglo girl and crushed his skull with a stone at the riverbank. But they'd already used the knife on her by then, on both of us. They thought it was funny that we should try to run away. A joke. So they toyed with us with their knives. I do not think they meant to kill us — we meant money to the sisters — but they were drunk and it was dark. The last I saw of my sister they were dragging her back across the river. I could not return for her unarmed but now I will. If I cannot have the horse and the rifle I will steal them somewhere else and go back and kill them until they kill me or else I will have my sister."

I don't think any of us knew what to say to that.

We just thought about it a while and passed the bottle.

"Out of curiousity, miss," Hart said finally. "How many you going up against?"

"Twelve, maybe fifteen and the three sisters. Unless there are buyers. There may very well be buyers. They began to clean us up the night before I left. In that case more. I would not know how many."

"Guards?"

"Only one. The settlement is in a canyon, hills north, south and west. They do not think they need more than one on the eastern side and a sentry on each hill. Though the guard from the night before last will still have a very bad headache, I think."

"Who are these buyers, exactly?" Mother asked.

"Brothel owners mostly. But also private clients, who are worse. The buyers don't matter. The one I kill first is Paddy Ryan."

"You mentioned that gentleman before, ma'am. Nasty sonovabitch with a letter *D* branded on his cheek, am I right?"

She nodded. Mother turned to me.

"Only thing in this godforsaken territory bigger and meaner than me. Hell, you probably wrote about him, Bell, and don't remember. Ryan was at Churubusco, one of those saintly Irish Catholic bastards from the San Patricio Battalion who went over to the Mex side. Damn near stopped old Scott in his tracks, too. And one of just seven who lived to tell about it. That *D* is for deserter, ma'am."

"I do remember him now. 'Course I do. At the court-martial not one soul would speak up against him."

"Would you? How could you be sure they'd hang him for you?"

I also remembered being told just a while ago that Hart had lost a brother at Churubusco. As Mother said, the deserters nearly turned the tide there. I wondered how he felt about that. Looking at him you couldn't say.

"So Ryan's pimping now," he said. "Found his god at last."

"I think he has many gods now," said Elena. "Not just money."

"How's that?"

"The sisters...they worship the Old Ones. Ryan does too, in his way."

"And who would these Old Ones be?"

"The old gods of Mexico. *Quetzalcoatl*, the Plumed Serpent. *Tezcatlipoca*, god of the moon and of the night. The sun god *Huitzilopochtli*. *Tlazolteotl,* Eater of Filth. *Xipe,* Lord of the Flayed. The old gods teach obedience. They teach resignation to the laws of earth and sky. Blood for bounty, blood for rain. Once the land oppressed us. Now men do. It is the same. For many of my people the Old Ones have never died. Why would they?"

In the sounds of these names I recognized the language I had heard her use last night by the fire — and felt the same chill at hearing it spoken again here. She'd told us of her father, a simple farmer. But I wondered who her mother had been and what terrible wisdom she'd imparted to her daughter.

"I told you of Ryan and the child at Garanta del Diablo. But I have seen worse."

"Like what?" said Hart.

"I have seen how my sister will die if she resists them. How she may already be dying. Because they will take their time. They always do."

We waited for more. But it wasn't forthcoming.

"Will you give me the horse and rifle?" she said.

We looked at one another across the fire.

"Mother?" Hart said. "It's your horse."

"It's your rifle," Mother said.

They nodded to her and handed her the whiskey and this time she drank.

† †

At sunrise we watched her saddle up and ride away. Watched until she was no more than a speck on the long empty horizon.

"You *sure* she don't remind you of somebody?" Mother said.

Hart twirled his dice awhile longer and then turned and dumped his coffee onto the fire.

"Damn you, Mother," he said.

NINE

We caught up to her as she crested a hill overlooking the Colorado.

If she was happy to see us you'd not have known it.

† †

We made our crossing.

We'd been lucky with the lack of rainfall of late so that there wasn't much current but Suzie and the other horses were pretty nearly swimming through the middle of it, hooves barely touching down and at times not touching down at all. On the other side we dismounted and unfastened the horse's girths and took off their saddles, allowing that they needed to get their wind back some after working so hard and I pulled my flask out of my saddlebag and passed it around and after a while we continued on.

By late midafternoon we'd reached a low flat ridge with sparse cover in the valley just beneath us and Elena stopped and pointed to the southwest.

"About half a mile," she said.

"All right," Hart said. "We'll head on down and wait till nightfall."

We started down slowly four abreast.

"You know where they're keeping her?" Hart said.

"Could be many places. Does it matter?"

"Unless you want to get us killed it might."

She seemed to consider that and then shrugged.

"It doesn't matter. I will find her."

Hart shook his head. She turned and studied him a moment.

"We don't get along too well, Mr. Hart. Why is that, do you think?"

"I respect what you want to do here, miss. It's family and I understand that. You're just goddamn sloppy going about it is all."

"That's not what I asked you."

"That's all you need to know about me and my being here, though."

"I don't think so."

"Look. Couple of years ago up to pretty recently I was spending a lot of time and giving a lot of thought to trying to kill you people so your people wouldn't kill me. It took some effort on my part but after a while I got real good at it. Now just because a few old men sign a piece of paper saying it's peacetime doesn't mean I all of a sudden feel all secure and happy in your company."

"I'm a woman, Mr. Hart."

"I'm well aware of that."

"You mean you saw me naked."

"That I did."

"So what did you see?"

"Nothing I haven't seen before and nothing real hard on the eyes particularly."

"You saw a Mexican. Half indian. You saw an enemy, right?"

"Maybe."

"Of course you did. You saw someone who is not like you. Someone who does not even pray to your Christian god.

He smiled. "That much, at least, I don't hold against you."

"I didn't fight the war."

"I never said you did."

"Mother tells me that you lost a brother."

"Oh, Mother does, does he?"

He shot Mother a look that could have burned saguaro into the steaming sand. Mother caught that look and apparently found an urgent need to study the sky.

"A stepbrother, yes."

"Ask me what I lost, Hart."

"Okay. What did you lose?"

She didn't much like his tone. I didn't much blame her.

"Fine," she said. "To hell with you. It's none of your damn business."

And it was only when we finally reached the grove of sheltering junipers below that I guess she changed her mind.

"A mother," she said. "That's all, Hart. To you, a Mex woman. Dead with a baby inside of her because the only doctor for five miles around was too busy with wounded Anglo *cabrones* like you and Paddy Ryan at the time. You killed women, Hart. You all did. Every last one of you."

TEN

We picketed the horses in the copse of trees and made our way through the scrub, the last few yards or so crawling on our bellies until we were within about forty yards of the compound and maybe ten yards from the lone guard in front who sat tending his small fire with sticks and twigs and gnawing on a half of roast rabbit, his rifle lying in the dirt beside him.

What I saw behind him in the sparks and waves of light pouring off the four huge bonfires might have come straight out of Dante's *Inferno* — a book I had never much liked in my youth — had Dante been a less than pious man.

"Well, we got us a hell of a party here," said Mother.

A marketing was taking place in front of us.

I saw perhaps thirty young women all grouped for inspection — the sisters' wares on display. Some simply standing shackled together and others bound to posts or wagon wheels, their clothing a bizarre mix of cheap shifts, men's shirts and trousers, dirty dresses and torn underwear or unrecognizable rags which barely even covered them, even a single stained ragged wedding dress among them. I saw drugged, beaten, half-crazy faces scrubbed newly clean for the buyers. I saw the buyers and their assistants, Mexican and Anglo, some well-dressed and some shabby-looking sweating in the heat of the bonfires, moving among them parting clothes and clutching at a bared breast or a crotch or buttocks, checking teeth and gums and laughing and talking amongst themselves.

I saw firearms everywhere.

We were not going up against twelve or fifteen men and three women. In fact there were only two women *not* on display that I could see — from Elena's description the younger sisters Maria and Lucia — moving from buyer to buyer like ranchers at a cattle show, doubtless talking prices.

But the men numbered well over two dozen.

"How good's their equipment?" Hart said.

"Their equipment?"

"Guns, rifles. How good are they?"

"Good, I think."

"Wait here. Won't be but a few minutes."

He turned and started crawling back the way we'd come, nobody thinking to question him and we lay there watching the milling crowd and listening to the crackling fires near and far.

"Why all the bonfires?" Mother asked her. "They light those damn things every night here?"

"Every night. To turn away the dark. To turn away the jungle and the creatures there."

Mother looked at her like she'd very possibly lost her mind and I suppose so did I.

We were staring out at barren dusty plain.

"Once all this was jungle. Many, many years ago. For the sisters it still is."

We were left to think on that and lie and watch until we heard a gentle rustling sound behind us and turned and there was Hart again crawling toward us through the brush, a horseblanket slung across his shoulder.

"Wait here," he said. "I won't be but a few minutes."

"You already said that," Mother said.

"Watch and learn, Mother."

He took off his hat and crushed the brim down and put it on again and wrapped the blanket around him serape-style and stood up big as you please and started slowly forward like there was nothing out of the ordinary to his being there at all. We heard the dice click in his hand and so did the guard sitting by the fire who lay the half-eaten rabbit down on a stump, wiped his greasy fingers on his shirt and picked up his rifle and stood.

"*Quien es?*" he said.

"*Que mosca ha picado?*"

"Eh?"

Hart sounded as bored and lazy as the guard did edgy and confused. Then it all came suddenly clear to him as Hart kicked him soundly between the legs so that he dropped the rifle and uttered a harsh strangled sound which Hart muffled with the palm of his hand and eased him to his knees and then picked up the rifle and gave him a good hard thump to the head with the butt end.

He dragged the man by one arm back over where we were lying, handed the rifle off to Mother and the blanket to me, turned him over and pulled his pistol out of his waistband.

".45 Peacemaker. Lady was right. Good equipment."

He pulled out his own ancient pistol and emptied the chambers.

"I'd try to sell this thing back to Gusdorf but I doubt he'd give me a penny for it. Should have buried it alongside his grandfather."

He tossed his old gun back into the bushes and holstered the new one.

"Feel better now?" said Mother.

"Much better."

"Glad to hear it. What about this fella?"

"Oh, he'll sleep some yet."

"No he won't," Elena said.

She lifted the guard's knife from his waistband and unsheathed it and before any of us even quite knew what she was up to her fingers were in his hair and she'd lifted his head and slit his throat as deftly as you'd slit a hog's and turned his head quickly off to the side so that the spill from his jugular flooded the earth beside us.

"Now *I* feel better," she said.

She looked up as though challenging us to say something but none of us were about to. Beyond whatever personal reasons she had and I thought they were probably very good ones you had to admit there was also a logic to it. One less pasteboard in the deck. One less reason to watch our backs. Hart nodded toward the settlement.

"You see your sister anywhere in there?"

"Yes. In the last group, over toward the hacienda. Celine is the one in white."

"I see her."

I spotted her too. A pretty girl of about fifteen or sixteen in a frayed white slip and camisole. I couldn't quite make out the look on her face from this distance whether strong or frightened though I tried. I seemed to want to know what the other half of this family was made of.

"You got anything on your mind at all about how we're gonna do this, Hart?" said Mother. "I mean, we can't just walk in and kick 'em *all* in the jewels, elegant though that was."

"Thank you, Mother. I got a notion might work."

We never did get to know what that was though because at just that moment the crowd went unexpectedly silent and we saw the doors to the hacienda open and walking through those doors — no, *gliding* through those doors like some Mexic witch on a broomstick was maybe the oldest woman I'd ever seen outside of a sickbed, a wild-haired grinning harridan draped in filmy white, long hanging breasts swaying back and forth beneath what she was wearing, a bleached skull crowning her head and her face painted in black streaks and circles over some dry clay-colored base. *Eva.* She carried a long black blade in front of her gripped in both hands. Its handle pointed toward the earth, its tip toward the sky.

By its size she should not even have been able to lift it.

The man behind her was painted too, a skull's face imposed over his own in stark black and white which gleamed in the flickering firelight. He was barechested and his chest and arms were massive. Around his waist he wore a belt of what appeared to be human bones. Humerus, radius, ulna. Around his neck, fangs or talons or both. I couldn't say.

In one hand he held a heavy leather leash and at the the end of it was a girl who might have been Celine's twin but for the large livid birthmark across her neck. Her dress was clean and white and looked new, a virgin's dress and she stumbled along behind him, her arms and face twitching on the razor's edge of some drug — pulque, mescal or some mix of their own divising, some powerful intoxicant.

"Ryan," Elena said.

"Christ on a crutch," Mother said. "Damned if it ain't. I'd never have known him."

"I'd have known him," said Hart.

For a moment all we heard was the crackling fires. Then the sisters began to chant. That same clicking, hissing tongue I'd heard Elena use only shrill this time. You thought of crickets dense in the still night air.

"Their *nahuatl*," she said. "Their prayer. The girl? The last time I saw her she was tied to a bed and screaming. I think her screams are over now."

"This is what I think it is?"

"Yes. To demonstrate obedience. To the sisters, to the old gods and the old ways. To show the buyers exactly what they are buying and what happens should they be fool enough to betray them."

"Why this girl?"

"I don't know. Probably she gave them trouble. Perhaps she was brave. Possibly she is not so valuable to them because of the mark."

The other two sisters, Maria and pug-faced Lucia, fell in behind them chanting as Eva and Ryan marched the girl through the guards and buyers and up the hill which glowed at its summit and billowed tarry smoke. Even the roughnecks among the crowd looking sober now and silent. At the top he turned the girl so that she faced the crowd and unbuttoned the front of her dress and parted it and Eva handed her the long obsidian blade and shouted to the crowd.

"*For Tezcatlipoca!*"

The girl hesitated, gazing at the knife in her hands in a kind of dazed twitching horror and then Ryan stepped forward and whispered something in her ear and to this day I still cannot imagine what it possibly could have been which would make her face seem suddenly to melt into that expression of beaten-down indifference as she turned the blade toward her and held it there a moment and then plunged it into her belly. Her eyelids flew open in shock and pain and her hands jerked reflexively off the hilt. Eva's hands replaced them and the long ropy muscles of her arms stood out through her flesh like crawling snakes as she sawed upward all the way to her breastbone and then pulled it gleaming out of her.

She began to fall, blood pulsing from the gaping wound and intestines beginning to ooze their way out of her, pale and red. Ryan took her by the shoulders.

"Do the rest of it!" he shouted. "Or dammit I'll give you right back to them. And I'll give you back *alive!"*

I could see her blinking rapidly, her body shuddering as in a blast of cold and we watched stunned and amazed — all but Elena I thought who must have known all along that this was coming — as the girl reached into the bloody cavity Eva had cut for her and dug out her own living heart steaming in the air and held it in her quaking hand. Eva snatched it from her like an eagle on a mouse and severed the arteries with a single quick stroke of the blade and held it to the crowd and shouted *Tezcatlipoca!* again and again as Ryan let go of her shoulders and the girl crumbled to her knees and I turned and delivered up my hardtack and coffee into the brush.

"Good a time as any, I'd say," said Hart. "Mother?"

He nodded. "Come on, Bell."

He pulled me up by the collar, my legs rubbery and weak and we skirted the periphery of the compound. I glanced over and saw that Ryan had the dead girl in his arms and was walking toward the fire-pit, his pants and naked belly slick with blood. I saw him raise her up over his head as though she weighed no more than a dog and saw old Eva place the bloodslick heart on the altar beside them. Then all I did was run.

ELEVEN

We were headed for the wide-open doors to the hacienda. I didn't know why or whose idea it was, Hart's or Elena's and perhaps the same thought had come to them both in some unspoken passage. But Elena knew full well that down to the very last guard they'd all be outside to witness the spectacle on the hilltop. The hacienda would be empty.

We climbed the stairs to the porch and ran inside through a short corridor and I barely had time to register the great elegant room we were in, bathed in candlelight as Elena marched us through and then pointed to the staircase.

"Up there."

"Why?" said Hart.

"The sisters' bedrooms. They'll make their deals inside, down in this room. We'll know when they start."

We took the stairs to the second-floor landing and walked a long wide carpeted corridor red as blood and studded with oil lamps in sconces past a door to our left and then stopped at the next one to our right and she opened it and we stepped inside.

The room was as big as Mother's entire cabin. A single lamp burned on a nighttable beside a beautiful mahogany canopied bed covered in lace. On its headboard was a carving of sheep being torn and devoured by a pack of wolves. Wolves adorned the finials on the bed and those atop the great swing mirror on the dressing table. I saw why she'd selected this room and not the one to our left. This one faced the yard. Through the windows you could see what was going on down there.

Should you want to.

"Maria's room," she said.

"I'll stay by the door," said Hart.

Elena pulled a velvet-backed walnut chair up to the window opposite him and sat with Hart's Winchester across her lap, watching.

Mother flopped down on the bed. It groaned beneath his weight.

I couldn't believe it. All I could do was look.

"I'm guessing it'll be a while yet. Am I right, ma'am?"

"Yes." Her voice was flat and cold.

"Have to take your rest where you find it, Bell."

He had a point I supposed. I suddenly felt exhausted, all we'd done and seen today a heavy weight upon me. I sat down at the foot of the bed beside him.

"I'd kill for a glass of whiskey," I said.

"On the sideboard," said Elena. "If you're fool enough."

I remember I did consider it. I truly did. It was tempting.

Instead I pulled a chair over to the side of the window opposite her and sat.

"Aren't you worried we'll be seen up here?" I said.

"We won't be seen. Look down there."

It was the second time that night a book I hadn't much cared for came to mind. The first was *Inferno*. This time it was Gibbon's *Decline and Fall of the Roman Empire*.

I was looking at an orgy.

In the moonlit firelit dust of the square I saw men and women coupling everywhere. Women spread out naked upon the bare red earth or on their knees being taken from behind, women sodomized and forced to perform fellatio. In more than one case both of these at the same time. I saw women being mauled and prodded and slapped and caned. And I saw guards and the three sisters passing through all of this and fueling its dementia with bottles of whiskey, mescal and tequila.

I was glad the window was shut so we didn't have to hear it too.

I saw joyless, spiritless faces. *Both the takers and the taken.*

It was when I saw what they were doing to Celine that I turned away.

✝   ✝

"You, writer," Elena had said to me the night before. *"Take this down.*

They will find it on our bodies."

✝   ✝

I don't wish to tell this. But I think I owe it to all concerned.

✝   ✝

"The fat pig is Fredo," she said. "The tall thin one is Gustavo. I do not know the third one. A buyer.

"You don't want to witness this, writer? Fine, don't."

But she wanted me to. I could hear it in her voice. I could see it in the eyes which pooled with tears but never wavered and barely blinked. When I saw what grief and rage those eyes held I turned back again.

If she could so could I.

Though Celine was directly below us had it not been for the thin white camisole pushed up nearly to her breasts I could not have recognized her. Her face was hidden.

She lay spread-eagled on her back naked from the camisole on down and the one Elena called Fredo was kneeling on each of her her forearms spread wide above her nearly at the elbow joint. Her head was in his cradled hands, raised up and tilted back toward him which must have agonized neck and arms and the muscles of her back as he moved her head up and down in time to his naked plunging hips. The Indio Gustavo held her legs apart at the ankles while the third man — an Anglo judging from his long thin matted hair — knelt to one side.

†   †

There was no way to know if the bird had been dead or alive when he began.

It was dead now.

Its head dangled in on a broken neck, wattles and comb and beak disappearing and reappearing again as he moved the hackles up inside her back and forth nearly up over the breastbone. He had the chicken gripped in both hands and when he looked up at Gustavo he was smiling.

"It is good," *she said.* "She will live through this. She does not resist. Soon, little sister. Soon."

I watched until the Anglo tired of this game and stood and walked over to where Gustavo was kneeling, dropped to his own knees in front of her, unbottoned his trousers and covered her with his body.

† †

An hour is a very long time to wait when you're frightened and know in your heart that something very bad is coming toward you like distant hoofbeats. Something that will likely change your life forever if you manage to live through it at all. You can deal with that hour in many different ways according to your lights.

Elena's gaze never left what was happening outside the window, the tension in her body visible only in her white-knuckled grip on the Winchester. Mother lay silent on the bed like a man dead in his casket with his hands folded over his belly and his eyes shut. Hart stood leaning against the wall behind the door, his rifle in one hand pointed at the floor and his dice rolling soundlessly across the knuckles of the other.

I sat there facing away from the window and closed my eyes and tried to stop wishing for a drink, tried to relax, tried to think about better days long past, theatre and the opera, baseball games and taverns with the boys at Harvard and my first love, Jane Geary, who left me for a Yalie for godsakes, blue skies fishing the Charles from over on the Cambridge side. But all that came to me instead were images from the Mexican campaign, the twisted broken bodies and hacked limbs foul and wet and pustulent with gangrene, heads cannon-shot five feet away from the bodies they belonged to and the shrieking of the newly wounded and long last sighs of the dying.

An hour is quite some time to wait.

And it was almost that long before I heard her say, *they're coming.*

Mother had not been asleep of course. Or if he was, deserted it as quickly as an eagle deserts its eyrie on sighting its prey below. At the sound of her voice he was up off the bed and flanking the door across from Hart and once again I was aware of the ease and grace of the man despite his huge size. Hart turned to Elena.

"The back door's where?"

"Straight down the hall to the right."

"You still see your sister out there?"

She nodded. "All of them. They're in one group now. Hobbled together."

"Men around her?"

"Just two."

"Good. When it starts, go out the back, get her and bring her round to the horses. These boys will want to get inside. We'll give 'em reason not to for a time. Then we'll follow you. You need any help?"

"No."

"You sure?"

"I'm sure."

"You ever shoot a man, Bell?"

"No."

"You're going to now. And I'm figuring it'll be mostly buyers in there and most of them'll be unarmed. You don't let that stop you, you hear me?"

I hesitated, then nodded.

"Hell, look at it this way," said Mother. "Suzie's got a tick? It's feeding off her blood? You take it 'tween thumb and forefinger. Then you squeeze. May not be pretty but that's what you do. It's the horse that's of consequence, not the goddamn tick."

"Our aim's to clear the room, Bell. That simple. Nobody stands but us when it's finished. That, and to watch each other's backs. Let's do it."

† †

I did not truly know war.

I knew it only by only its consequences. But as we walked the stairs, Hart and Mother in front and Elena and I behind, I felt what I imagine any soldier must feel who though not yet having engaged in battle is not wholly ignorant of those consequences. Fear, yes, of course fear. A clear ringing signal from mind to body that quickens the heartbeat, deadens the legs and thickens and dries the throat so that it was nearly impossible to swallow. Of course fear. But also a hammering dread, a great overwhelming *reluctance*. I was about to risk my life for the single awful purpose of taking the lives of others — and as many lives as possible. And what sane man would wish to do either.

Our aim's to clear the room, Bell.

I long ago knew that war was insanity.

What I did not know was the exact nature of how that insanity was made manifest in a single soul.

For a moment it seemed incredible to me that I should even be here.

That feeling of displacement grew with each step I took to the extent that I could only dimly register the laughter and talk coming from the room we were approaching below and smell the cigar smoke until finally we reached the landing and the open wide double doors and Hart and Mother stepped inside and raised their rifles to astonished faces all around and I stood at Mother's side with Elena to the right and then the feeling fled like a dove from a flame as we began firing.

I saw the fat woman Lucia go down like a toppled sack of grain with a bullet from Elena's rifle before I had even sighted and pulled the trigger on the bearded Mexican in the tailored suit directly in front of me. His move for cover came too late. My bullet caught him in the chest.

I did not then think *I have killed, I have just killed a human being.* I doubt I thought anything. It was as unconsidered a response as a cat lashing out after a mouse in front of him scurrying across the floor. I just kept shooting.

There were shouts and men screaming and in that enclosed space the deafening staccato bursts of rifles and I was aware that while Hart had been correct, that most of these men were unarmed, a few were shooting back at us with pistols so that they became the nexus points of all our senses, Hart and I firing simutaneously at a dirty long-haired Anglo who might have been the one we saw on top of Celine outside the window. He pitched back into a slim side table which shattered beneath his weight and fired wild into the ceiling, raining the others with crystal glass from the chandelier.

Mother shot a man who looked like a gambler from the way he dressed and who fired at him with a four-barrel pepperbox even after it was empty.

The woman Maria had two men standing in front of her, presumably both guards, one whose pistol remained holstered, his hands already in the air and one firing at me in panic and missing wide. Mother blew him back to where Maria would have stood had she not been on the move already, throwing open the rolltop desk behind her, snatching up the pistol inside and firing at Elena. I could hear the bullet pass like a mosquito in flight and saw Elena's cheek sprout a sudden line of blood as she sighted the woman down and fired.

Men were falling all around us, only a few left standing and none of them armed by now but for the guard with his hands in the air. I shot one of them twice in the back as he made for the front window to my left. I saw Maria stumbling trying to stand and firing at Elena though by then she was shot in each thigh. Elena sighted once again and squeezed and her face disappeared beneath a bright red flower of blood and bone.

Mother shot the guard who'd surrendered.

The bullet shattered a thin china vase behind him.

Elena and Hart walked to where a dirty young Mexican man was cowering crying and praying in short breathy gasps beneath the long narrow table in the center of the room and Hart shoved away the table with the sole of his boot and Elena pointed her rifle down and shot him at the base of the neck.

And then for a moment there were only the moans of the dying and the echos of our rifles like waves pounding a nearby shore and gunpowder drifting thick on the still air, watering our eyes and tasting of copper and brimstone in our mouths.

† †

Then the window shattered. Bullets slammed into the wall behind us.

† †

Mother was reloading and so was I, frantically. My hands were shaking and I couldn't seem to grip the bullets and feed them into the chamber. We heard footfalls coming toward us on the steps outside and men cursing. Hart drew his pistol and stepped past the bodies to the room's front door. He turned to Elena. *Go! now!* he shouted and stepped out into the hallway and his Peacemaker roared as she turned and ran.

A moment later Mother and I were beside him.

TWELVE

I became a ghost, she said.

*I watched in the shadows between the two outbuildings
to the left of the hacienda as the men stumbled out the
doorway and down the steps under your fire and Paddy Ryan
in his death mask strapped on a pistol and gave the order to
pull a wagon between the window and front doorway on the
left and another to the windows on the right for cover. Drunk
or not, stupid or not they did this quickly and by then you
were firing through the front windows and I knew I had little
time, that it would not be long before Ryan sent some of his
men to the rear door to cut off your retreat. When he did
they would have no trouble seeing me here.*

*Celine and the others were on their knees or trying to
crawl away but hobbled close together as they were there
was nowhere they could really go. To get to them I needed
to cross twenty yards of open space past a bonfire still
burning low but there was no help for that so I pulled the*
soldado*'s good sharp knife from my belt and made my run.*

I knelt in front of her and all she said was sister! *startled,
as I cut through the ropes at her feet and all I said was* come,
hurry! *as I drew her to her feet and pushed her out ahead of*

me toward the mouth of the canyon and handed the knife to the Anglo girl beside her and perhaps that was my mistake. Perhaps the other girls freeing themselves one by one was what drew their attention first to them and then to us because as we neared the dead guard's smoldering campfire Celine stumbled to the ground or so I thought and clutched at her hip and I saw that she was shot, blood seeping through the dirty white slip.

I hauled her up and wrapped her arm about my neck and over my shoulder and moved her past the fire into the brush. I glanced back and saw Paddy Ryan staring straight at me, straight in the eye, saw his look of recognition and he pointed to me and shouted, then pointed to the rear of the hacienda directing his men toward the back.

And then he and three of the others were running after us. We ducked into the brush but my sister stumbled again and cried out in pain. The bullet had either chipped her hipbone or perhaps hit a nerve or both. I pulled her to her feet again and now I was half dragging her. We were not going to make it to the horses.

I could practically smell Paddy Ryan behind us.

Her leg was weak but not her arms I thought. Can you climb? *I asked her. We were coming to a stand of trees beyond the fires' glow and it was dark.* Celine, can you climb? I think so, *she said. She managed to give me a brave frightened smile.* I always could. This one, *I said.* Use the good leg. Jump. *I put my hands around her waist gone so slim I could feel her ribs like the hoops of a barrel and pushed her up. She caught hold of a limb. I pushed at the sole of her boot and she was up and climbing through the branches and I saw her wince in pain. I slung the rifle over my shoulder and followed.*

Moments later we heard them below and I could only pray to all the gods, your own included that they were neither

Indios nor night hunters and would not look up because although I had unslung the rifle I could probably shoot two of them or maybe even three but I was not going to shoot them all before they shot me. We were lucky. They continued on.

Toward the horses.

And a few moments later returned with them — the horses snorting, disliking the heavy clinging scrub they were being led through and I heard Paddy Ryan laugh and say like to see how far they get without these *and then shout as he passed the dying campfire,* see you in the morning, ladies, *knowing we had to be nearby.*

When were were certain they were gone I helped my sister down.

It was quiet. The shooting had stopped. When I didn't know.

We waited for you.

THIRTEEN

"You think she's had time?" Mother said.

"She'd damn well better have," said Hart.

"You figure we wore out our welcome here?"

"That I do."

There were three guards dead in the hallway from their first blind rush at us but we hadn't done much outside. I counted them at twelve or thirteen firing from behind or under the wagons. Rifle fire kept pouring through the windows. It was hard to get a shot in much less aim effectively. We ran for the back door. Midway down the hall I glanced over my shoulder and saw a dark shape coming toward us and I fired off a round in that direction and then kept running.

† †

Ten steps further and we'd have made it to the door.

Ten steps less and we could have turned into one of the open rooms on either side.

Instead fortune trapped us there in the hallway with six rifles to our three.

† †

I took the first hit like a fist to the thigh at the same time two of the guards went down beneath our fire and Mother took the second just above his hip and the then a third square in the chest yet amazingly remained standing, only stumbled back behind me still firing, the three of us moving slowly forward pressed back against the walls, dropping two more men in the doorway while the two remaining backed on out over the threshold, turning their rifles in and firing wild and blind, Hart unsheathing the Peacemaker and blasting great splintered gouges out of the casing trim on either side until we were almost there and I heard a sound come out of Mother unlike any a man should ever hear.

I turned and so did Hart as Mother's rifle hit the floor and we saw something the size of a railroad spike protruding from his neck. And then seeming to try to *withdraw* from his neck, moving side to side and up and down as though it were a living thing there trying to wriggle free, Mother's hands fisted and grasping at it as though to keep it a part of him instead, his eyes wide and blood pouring like thick bright syrup down off his mouth onto his chest and tides of it pulsing against the wall.

He shifted his weight and there was old mad Eva behind him — tiny in his shadow, some horrible gnome who would bring a giant low — grasping at the hilt of her obsidian blade with both bony hands and trying to wrest it out of him, her lips snarled back in a feral grin, eyes squinting and twitching as though she were trying to focus on something far away in blinding light until Hart stepped over and shot directly into one of those rheumy yellow eyes and painted the wall with whatever manner of filth had come to nestle in her brain.

She lay still and I saw what the white filmy garment was which left her long thin dugs and cascades of belly flesh so nearly and revoltingly naked.

Flayed human skin.

Mother fell to his knees. His hands dropped away from the dagger and his arms swayed at his sides. He seemed to gaze at Hart for a moment with puzzlement and then with slow recognition and that was all.

His weight shifted back.

He hung there perfectly still.

I did not think at that moment about how Mother had cared for me, taught me. I did not think that as one is wont to love another man I perhaps had loved this one. That would come only later. I saw a dead man. Mother was fled.

"Aw jesus, Mother," said Hart.

The gunfire outside had stopped. The men had retreated from the doorway and as yet we had no notion why. It didn't seem reasonable. All they had to do now was come at us from both ends of the hallway if they did it quick enough. We could retreat into one of the rooms but couldn't hold out there forever. They'd lose some men doing it that way but they'd surely have us sooner or later.

I was aware of a tingling climbing down my leg. Not gone numb as yet but it felt as though it very well could given time. Above the wound it throbbed.

"Can you manage, Bell?" he said.

I nodded. I looked at the dead man kneeling before me and didn't trust myself to speak.

I saw that Hart had been shot high in the side of his chest. I didn't want to address that either. There was a lot of blood.

"We best try to get out of here."

We stepped over the four bodies in the doorway and headed for the outbuidings — expecting gunfire all the way.

87

Gunfire that never came. We skirted the buildings into the brush and beyond to the clearing where we'd tethered the horses. But of course there were no horses.

Only Elena and Celine in open moonlight.

† †

"Mother?" said Elena.

Hart didn't answer. Didn't need to. His look was enough. His eyes were pure dark flint and she took his glance like a physical blow. I could almost feel her thinking, *this man blames me. Of course he does. He blames me for for the loss of his friend.*

It was certainly possible. You couldn't know. Sometimes you just couldn't read him.

Her response was to get busy. She gestured toward me. *"Ayudame, Celine,"* she said, *"este uno."*

Celine walked with a bad limp and I could see where she'd been hipshot and the hem of her slip torn off for a bandage, something brownish beneath the bandage which I learned by repeating the process later on myself was a simple mix of dirt and her own urine — but the next thing I knew she was opening my pants and rolling them gently down over my hip to get at the wound while Elena drew Hart's shirt off over his shoulders. He'd been hit just under the armpit, the bullet passing through the tissue between chest and underarm front and back. The bleeding was largely stopped by now but there'd already been a lot of it.

"So you're Celine," I said.

The words sounded stupid even as I uttered them. I may even have been close to shock, I don't know. But I seemed to need to say something. Here was this pretty young Mexican girl dabbing at my naked thigh with a strip of cloth torn from her slip. Another inch or two and I'd have no secrets at all from her.

"I don't know how to thank you," she said.

She looked at Hart. "Both of you."

Hart's expression went from a grimace to something nearly a smile.

"They'll expect us to run," he said. "Probably come after us at first light. They'll figure it'll be easy, with us on foot. So you want to thank me, girl? How are you at horse stealing?"

FOURTEEN

I doubt any of us slept at all that night. I know I didn't. Wouldn't have even if my wounded thigh had let me. And when, in the darkest hour, just before sunrise, the hour of the wolf, they call it, Hart touched my shoulder to rouse me I was as ready as I ever would be.

We returned by way of the scrub, skirting the guard's dead campfire, much as Hart and I had come the night before, Celine and I with difficulty, through a light steady rainfall and by dawn we were crouched in the dripping brush with a full view of Paddy Ryan sitting in a rocking chair on the porch, scrubbed clean of his black and white makeup and drinking from a dainty china cup.

We saw two guards each in front of the pair of outbuildings to our right which led us to presume the remaining captives were housed within, three more in the corral feeding and currying the horses and another in the center of the compound near the well. Finally, the men Elena called Fredo and Gustavo stood with their backs to us in front of a wagon wheel directly ahead tossing rocks and pebbles at something and laughing.

When they stooped down to collect more stones and pebbles we saw what it was.

† †

I'd heard of it during the war.

It was not only heart, tongue or genitals the guerrillas might take from a man.

There were times they took his brain.

And there was Mother tied spreadeagled to the wagon wheel. The top of his head was sawn away just above the eyebrows and it was into this cavity, empty now but for rainwater, that the men were pitching their stones.

† †

Elena touched Hart's shoulder.

"Hart," she said.

He didn't answer. Only stared out at the men, the dice clutched tight in his fist.

"Hart. I'm so sorry."

"Why's that?"

"*Please*, Hart. Please."

I thought she was about to cry. *Elena, about to cry.* It was almost as shocking as what was going on in front of us. But then he turned to her and for the first time when he spoke to her his voice was gentle.

"I'd never hold it against you, ma'am. And neither would he. Like I said, it's family. Everybody's got family."

And for a moment I saw something pass between them, something true and almost tender made of respect and loss and suffering and she nodded to him and he said softly *even me* and turned his gaze back to the yard.

To the sounds of Fredo and Gustavo laughing in the yard.

Tossing their stones.

Even me he said again and this time you could feel the heat of all his anger in the words. We watched in silence for a while.

"I count eleven," I said. "Spread out all over the place. It'll be rough getting to those horses."

"We aren't going for the horses."

"Huh?"

"Mother just changed plans for me."

I looked at him. He sighed.

"Bell, you're a lot better man than you think you are. At least when you're sober. But you're not gonna be doing any running on that leg for quite a while yet and neither is this young girl. We're not going after any horses. Hold these for me minute, will you?"

He handed me the dice. He unholstered his pistol, opened it and spun the chamber, closed it and reholstered it and then turned to Elena.

"I'd like my Winchester back now if it's all the same to you, ma'am. And if I could borrow your knife."

I think we all knew what he was thinking by then and Elena looked reluctant to acceed to his wishes. I didn't blame her one bit.

"You've still got Bell's rifle. And his sidearm."

"A pistol's not good for much of anything at this range, Hart," I said. "You know that."

"Be that as it may."

He held out his hand.

She handed him the knife which he slipped into his belt and then the rifle. He checked the load and placed it down next to the one he'd taken off the guard and stripped off his shirt. He propped the Winchester up against his chest and tied it in place with his shirtsleeves and then picked up the other rifle.

"See you," he said. Then stood up and started walking. Not hurrying, just walking — and I thought of the story about Hart and the stolen cattle and felt something leap inside me that was at once glad to know that I had lived to see this man this day and fearful for its outcome.

"Give me your pistol, Bell," Elena said and I did.

I don't know what it was that made them turn, some intuition or some signal from the other guards which they were able to see but we didn't but Fredo and Gustavo whirled on him nearly as one. It was too late all the same. Hart pumped two bullets into Fredo's fat belly and a third into Gustavo's chest before they could get off a single shot and then walked to where Fredo lay rolling on the ground and put a fourth bullet into his ear.

He moved to Mother and cut him down and laid him gently on the ground.

I heard Ryan yelling something from the porch, standing with his hand in the air, telling his people to hold off.

Hart knelt there mostly obscured by the wagon and reloaded.

Then he was up again and walking into what my heart told me was going to be a vicious line of fire like he was taking a stroll on a sunny day. The moments seemed to stretch and expand, time all out of whack. He was waging a war of nerves here. It was a war that the man standing at the well lost first, his shot going wide. Hart aimed and fired and the man went down. Then all hell broke loose, Hart still that slow-moving target, bullets kicking up muddy dirt all around.

I'd already picked my man, exposed in the corral over by the horses. I fired at him and missed the first and second time but not the third.

There were horses between me and the other two men so I looked for a better target and saw Hart moving toward the outbuildings, taking one of the men down at the first building and then whirling and firing toward the second and I had a clear shot at one of the guards there too so I fired and Hart fired and have no idea which of our bullets cut him down.

The remaining two men at the outbuildings had hidden behind wooden water barrels when the shooting started but Hart kept marching toward them. I saw him throw away the first rifle and tear the Winchester off his chest and fire into nearest barrel over and over again while I followed suit with the second, aware suddenly that Elena was not beside me — Celine was, but not her sister — and for a moment I thought she'd been shot though that was hardly likely and then I considered it no further but concentrated on the man behind the barrel.

I saw Hart take a bullet in the thigh and side almost simultaneously. They staggered but didn't stop him and he was nearly on top of the first barrel when the man slid away limp behind it under his fire. He turned toward the second. I needed to stop to reload. As I fumbled with the cartridges I saw him toss down the Remington and pull out his pistol as a bullet hit him low in the shoulder and spun him down to the mud.

I saw Ryan smiling from the porch, the heavy oak door his cover.

His shot, his bullet.

Hart was like a bull in a corrida now, managing only to get to his knees as still another bullet took him in the thigh again and I thought, *Christ, it's not a corrida it's a goddamn slaughterhouse* as another slapped into his chest and yet another into his upper arm, that arm his gunhand so that he could barely raise the gun enough to switch it to the other hand but switch hands he did and fired into the corral and I could see one of the men fall beneath the panicked horses' hooves and I went back to my barrel again and finally the man behind it was aware of the angle and direction of my fire and ignored Hart for a moment and turned to aim at me and when he did I put a bullet into his chest.

Hart had turned to fire at Ryan and now I saw why. The third man in the corral lay as dead as the other two and that left only Ryan. There was a puzzled look on Hart's face that told me it wasn't Hart who had shot the man.

I did as he did, slamming bullets into the old oak door until it barely even looked like a door anymore, just a tall dark rectangle of ruined hacked wood but my rifle was about as ineffective penetrating the thing at this range as Hart's Peacemaker and Ryan wouldn't show his face and finally I had to reload again.

And realized that so did Hart.

† †

I don't know why I did what I did then.

As I've said, I'm not a brave man.

And I am not generally given to foolish endeavors.

But suddenly I could no longer stand to see Hart out there on his knees while I remained in cover. I stepped out of the scrub and concentrated on reloading and not the pain shooting through my leg or even Ryan for that matter aware only that for the moment at least the firing had ceased on both sides as I stumbled limping toward him and managed to get one bullet and then two into the rifle and I was no more than ten feet away when the firing started once again and I felt something slap my head like I'd run into the limb of a tree and it whirled me away to the ground and then I was tasting mud in my mouth and blood and then the next thing I saw was Hart take still another shot to the chest throwing him down, the two of us lying practically side to side.

I looked up and saw Ryan come off the porch smiling, wearing the look of a man happier to kill than eat, saw him glance first dismissively at me and then walk up to Hart with his pistol raised and I heard Hart say *you worthless piece of horshit, you're dead, you know that?* and you could see it suddenly dawn on the man that against all odds or reason it was true just as Elena who had come out from behind the outbuilding and was now only three or four steps behind him blew out the back of his head, shattering his face and pitching him into the mud.

I attempted to move.

"Stay still," she said. "You're head-shot, Bell."

She went to Hart and knelt beside him.

"You might have let me help right from the beginning," she said.

"You did help."

"You know what I mean."

"It's all right. There's nothing I'd have wished to do differently."

"You're a fool, Hart."

"Not a kind thing to say to a dying man, Elena."

"I'm sorry."

"Don't be."

"I was only just beginning to like you, Hart."

"I don't know why you would," he said. "But thank you, ma'am."

97

FIFTEEN

We crossed this time at Gable's Ferry. That meant we had to travel north a ways but we didn't want to risk the river with our burden. Old Man Gable had hired help by then and the boy who ran the ferry wasn't happy to see us wounded as we were and bearing two shot corpses. A few of the girls from the compound were with us. He seemed to like their company much better.

I wasn't hardly fit for digging nor was Celine so it was Elena who buried them out behind our corral. A shady spot on a little hill where the wind would whistle by on an autumn afternoon and we marked their graves with two crosses cut from wood off the corral itself since it was Mother who had built it. Again it was Elena who pushed and then hammered them deep into the fresh-turned earth.

"Want to say something, Marion Bell?"

I thought for a moment. "I don't know what to say. They were my friends. The best I ever knew. Best a man could want, I think. So I guess that's what I'll say. They were my friends."

She looked at Celine.

"Brave men. Kind men and generous. I won't forget them."

Then Elena did a surprising thing. She produced a small tattered bible from the folds of the skirt she'd made for the occasion. I recognized it to be Mother's.

I had never seen him read or even open it.

"*'Ye are the light of the world,*" she read. *"A city that is set on a hill cannot be hid. Neither do men light a candle, and put it under a bushel, but on a candlestick; and it giveth light to all that are in the house. Let your light so shine before men, that they may see your good works, and glorify your Father which is in heaven.'* Book of Matthew. Amen."

I wept and later, as they left me, sat down to write.